Baby Bunny's EASTER Surprise

Helen Baugh
Illustrated by Nick East

HarperCollins *Children's Books*

On Easter morning, baby Letty raised her **sleepy head.**

She opened up one big brown eye,
then **hopped** straight out of bed.

Baby Bunny's EASTER Surprise

To Charlotte and Ella xx
H. B.

For Pixie Poppy Dean and all the Easter eggs x
N. E.

First published in paperback in Great Britain by HarperCollins *Children's Books* in 2022

HarperCollins *Children's Books* is a division of HarperCollins*Publishers* Ltd
1 London Bridge Street, London SE1 9GF

www.harpercollins.co.uk

HarperCollins*Publishers*
1st Floor, Watermarque Building, Ringsend Road, Dublin 4, Ireland

1 3 5 7 9 10 8 6 4 2

Text copyright © Helen Baugh 2022
Illustrations copyright © Nick East 2022

ISBN: 978-0-00-850295-9

Printed in Great Britain by Bell and Bain Ltd, Glasgow

MIX
Paper from
responsible sources
FSC™ C007454

This book is produced from independently certified FSC™ paper
to ensure responsible forest management.

For more information visit: www.harpercollins.co.uk/green

HOPPY EASTER

BOING

She'd seen her mummy's cotton-tail –
so fluffy, clean and white –
quiver quickly by the door,
then **disappear** from sight!

Letty knew she must move fast. She had to make it **snappy!**

She shook her **flippy-floppy ears**

and hoisted up her **nappy.**

If she was to be the first to find the Easter eggs,
she had to keep up with her mummy,
on her **little legs**.

You see, Letty had a secret ...
something **wonderful** and funny ...

...she'd found out that her **mummy** was the real-life

Easter Bunny!

The Easter Bunny hid her **first** egg
halfway up a tree.
It was green with pale-pink spots
and it was **very** hard to see!

But Letty hopped straight to it,
quite **devoted** to her cause.

In **two shakes** of a bunny's tail,
the egg was in her paws.

Now, little Letty knew
the Easter egg
was **not** for her,

but she **sniffed** it
as she held it close
against her soft, brown fur.

SNIFF
SNIFF

One sniff was all it took!
Her small nose wrinkled in delight!
The chocolate smelled so good!
She'd have to take a tiny bite.

CRUNCH

So Letty had a teeny-weeny, titchy taste. Just one.
It was SUPER-CHOCCYLICIOUS!
And next thing . . .

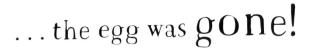

…the egg was **gone!**

Oh, Letty!

"Oops!" she said. "I couldn't stop!
The egg was scrummy yummy!
And no one else will know
because it's **hidden** in my tummy!"

But Letty had some chocolate
on the tip of her sweet nose.
And flakes of chocolate on her whiskers -
quite a lot of those!

The Easter Bunny hid her **next** eggs
on a pond close by.
They were blue with yellow stripes
and they were **very** hard to spy!

But Letty hopped straight to them,
quite **devoted** to her cause.

In two shakes of a bunny's tail,
both eggs were in her paws.

Now, little Letty knew
the Easter eggs
were **not** for her,

HAPPY
EASTER,
DUCK

HAPPY
EASTER,
FROG

but she sneaked
a **peep** inside them
as they lay against her fur.

One **peep** was all it took!
Her brown eyes widened in delight!
The chocolate looked so **tempting**!
She would have to take a bite.

So Letty had a teeny-weeny, titchy taste. Just one.
It was DOUBLE-CHOCCYLICIOUS!
And next thing . . .

. . . the eggs were gone.

Oh, Letty!

"Oops!" she said. "I couldn't stop!
The eggs were scrummy yummy!
And no one else will know
because they're **hidden**
in my tummy!"

But Letty had a smudge of melted chocolate on her chin . . .
and gooey chocolate on her cheek, with pretty sprinkles in.
Plus, of course, the chocolate on the tip of her sweet nose.
And the flakes upon her whiskers –
there were quite a lot of those!

The Easter Bunny hid **more** eggs
on top of toadstools tall.
They were red and white and dotty.
It was **hard** to see them all!

But Letty hopped straight to them,
quite **devoted** to her cause.

In two shakes of a bunny's tail,
three eggs were in her paws.

Now, little Letty knew
the Easter eggs were **not** for her,

.but she **shook** them
up and down
as they lay close against
her fur.

One **shake** was all it took!
Her ears flipped straight up in delight!
She'd heard some **treats** inside
and now she'd have to take a bite.

So Letty had a teeny-weeny, titchy taste. Just one.
It was TRIPLE-CHOCCYLICIOUS!
And next thing . . .

. . . the eggs were gone.

OH, LETTY!

"Oops!" she said. "I couldn't stop!
The eggs were scrummy yummy!
And no one else will know
because they're hidden
in my tummy!"

But Letty had a chocolate treat stuck on one floppy **ear**.
Above her big brown **eyes** there was a big brown chocolate smear.

Then there was the smudge of melted chocolate on her **chin**,
and the gooey chocolate on her **cheek** with pretty sprinkles in.
Plus, of course, the chocolate on the tip of her sweet **nose**.
And the flakes upon her **whiskers** –
there were quite a lot of those!

Soon Letty heard some hop-hop-hops.
Oh no! It was her mummy!
Stay calm! she thought. *She will not know
the eggs are in my* tummy!

But Mummy took one look at Letty,
then she shook her head.
"Those eggs were not for you,
my baby bunny," Mummy said.

"I'm sorry!" Letty cried. "I didn't mean to eat them all! It's hard to NOT eat Easter eggs when you are very small."

Mummy licked her paw and gently cleaned up Letty's face.
"Come on," she said.
"Let's put new eggs in each old hiding place."

So Letty and her mummy
took new eggs **back** to the tree,

to the pond and to the toadstools
- they hid **one**, then **two**,
then **three**.

The basket was now empty.
There were **no** more eggs. Not one.
And Letty's ears flopped downwards
when she saw that they were **gone**.

"Mummy," Letty whispered, speaking softly as can be.
"You've hidden eggs for everyone . . .
but you've forgotten me."

"I'll NEVER forget you," her mummy said. "Now, close your eyes."
And Letty hopped with happiness
when her friends cried . . .